SPOOKY GHOST STORIES FOR KIDS 6-12

AWESOME SPINE-TINGLING TALES FOR HALLOWEEN AND ALL YEAR ROUND

TED ALDWICK

CONTENTS

THE WHISPERING WALLS

HAVE YOU EVER HEARD A WALL SPEAK? LUCY had just moved into an ancient house, and her bedroom was unlike any she'd ever seen. It was large, with blue peeling paint and walls covered in elegant, faded wallpaper.

The first night, as she snuggled into her bed, Lucy heard soft, indistinct murmurs. "It's just the wind," she told herself, pulling the covers over her head. But each night, the whispers grew louder and clearer.

"Find the locket...save the memory..." the voices pleaded. They didn't sound scary, more like they were trapped and needed help. Curious, Lucy decided to find out where the sounds were coming from.

One day, while pressing her ear against different parts of the wall, Lucy found a loose piece of wallpaper. Slowly, she peeled it back to reveal a hidden compartment. Inside was an old, dusty locket with a faded picture of a young girl, almost Lucy's age, with twinkling eyes and a soft smile.

That evening, as the sun dipped and the room darkened, Lucy clasped the locket in her hand. The whispers grew excited, "Thank you...you found it!" Suddenly, in the dim light, the ghostly figure of the girl in the locket appeared before Lucy. She wasn't scary, just translucent and shimmering.

"I'm Eliza," she said softly. "This was my room a long time ago. I lost my locket, and with it, my favorite memory of my family. But now that you've found it, I can move on. Thank you, Lucy."

With a smile and a nod, Eliza's figure faded away, leaving Lucy in awe. From that day on, the walls were silent, but Lucy knew she had made a special friend in Eliza and that her new room held secrets of the past, waiting to be discovered.

SHADOWS IN THE ATTIC

HAVE YOU EVER SEEN YOUR REFLECTION MOVE on its own? Jack hadn't, until he discovered an old, ornate mirror covered in cobwebs in the corner of his attic. He'd been playing there, exploring hidden treasures, when the glint of the mirror's frame caught his eye.

Curiously, he wiped away the grime and saw his own reflection staring back. But as Jack shifted, the mirror displayed more than just his movements. Other figures began to emerge in the glass, casting shadows that danced and swirled. They looked like people, but not anyone Jack knew.

The first was a tall man in a top hat, then

a woman in a flowing gown, and a little boy with a toy train. As Jack watched, mesmerized, the shadows acted out scenes from their lives, laughing, dancing, and playing.

Each night, Jack sneaked into the attic to witness more stories from the past. The shadows seemed to be sharing the history of everyone who had once lived in the house. It was magical, but Jack couldn't shake the feeling that they wanted something.

One evening, as Jack was engrossed in the shadowy tales, he noticed a figure that looked eerily familiar: a boy, his age, with the same mop of curly hair. The shadow boy pointed towards Jack and then at the back of the mirror.

Heart pounding, Jack investigated and found a loose panel. Inside was a diary. It belonged to a boy named Samuel who'd lived in the house a century ago. The last entry read: "*The mirror shows many things, but it's lonely. It seeks a friend*."

Suddenly, Jack's reflection in the mirror smiled, while he stood frozen in shock. He realized the mirror was indeed lonely and wanted to keep him as its new shadow friend.

Jack fled the attic, never to return. He told his parents, and the mirror was covered up, its tales and shadows concealed for good. But Jack never forgot the night the mirror tried to claim him.

THE MIDNIGHT GAME

EVER PLAYED A GAME YOU LATER REGRETTED? On a stormy night, Mia and her friends decided to play "The Midnight Game" during their sleepover. They'd heard of it, an old legend that promised to summon a ghost if done correctly.

With a single candle as their light, they sat in a circle, each writing down a wish on a piece of paper. The legend said that if they chanted the ghost's name three times at the stroke of midnight, their wishes would come true. But, there was a catch; the ghost was known to be mischievous and might twist their wishes in unexpected ways.

Midnight approached, and the chimes of

a distant clock began. As they chanted, the room grew colder, and their candle flickered before going out. A chilling breeze swirled around them, rustling the wishes they'd written.

Suddenly, shadows danced on the walls, and a soft giggle echoed. "Who dares to call me?" whispered a playful voice.

Mia gulped. "We do. We want our wishes granted."

The ghost giggled again. "Very well, but remember, all wishes come with a price."

One by one, their wishes began to come true, but not as they expected. Mia's wish for endless chocolate turned her room into a messy chocolate swamp. Her friend Zoe's wish for invisibility made only her clothes disappear, much to her embarrassment. And Jake, who wished to fly, found himself floating like a balloon, unable to come down.

The kids panicked, realizing their error. "Please, we didn't mean any harm. Can you undo our wishes?" Mia pleaded.

The mischievous ghost laughed, "Always be careful with wishes. But since it's your first time, I'll help you out." With a snap, everything returned to normal.

As dawn broke, the sleepover gang promised never to play "The Midnight Game" again. But they'd always remember the night their wishes went hilariously wrong.

THE HAUNTED DOLLHOUSE

HAVE YOU EVER WONDERED IF TOYS HAVE secrets? Anna always wanted a dollhouse. On her 9th birthday, she got one - an old, intricate model passed down from her grandmother. This wasn't just any dollhouse; it was an exact replica of Anna's own home.

Every evening, Anna would lovingly set up the miniature furniture and place the tiny dolls in various rooms. She'd imagine wonderful tales of the doll family residing within. But as night fell and Anna went to bed, peculiar things began to happen.

From her bed, she'd hear faint whispers, the clinking of tiny dishes, and even the creaking of miniature doors. Curiosity overcoming fear, she decided one night to stay awake and observe the dollhouse.

To her amazement, the dolls moved! Mirroring her family's daily life, the tiny figures enacted scenes from the day. Anna saw herself playing in her room, her mom cooking in the kitchen, and her dad reading in the living room. It was enchanting, yet eerie.

But things took a chilling turn when Anna witnessed a shadowy figure she didn't recognize. It lurked outside the miniature home, peeking through windows and rattling doors. Panicking, Anna turned on the lights and the eerie reenactment stopped.

Determined to solve the mystery, Anna asked her grandmother about the dollhouse. Her grandmother's face turned pale. She spoke of an ancestor who, many years ago, built the real house and its doll-sized replica. A jealous rival, wishing to claim the land, was always lurking, trying to find a way in. But he never succeeded. This bitter man, it seemed, was now trapped in the dollhouse realm, forever trying to enter the home he so coveted.

Anna placed a tiny fence and locked doors around the dollhouse, hoping to keep the shadowy figure out. But every night, she'd still hear the faint attempts of the figure trying to get in. However, with her protective measures, Anna and her family inside the dollhouse remained safe. But she always wondered, what if he finds a way into the real house?

Ghostly Footprints

Have you ever followed footprints to a mysterious end? In the small town of Willowbrook, every morning, a trail of wet footprints would appear leading from the center of town to the edge of the placid, blue lake. No one knew where they came from or why they were there. The footprints were bare, as if someone had walked straight out of the water and into the heart of town.

The town's children were the most curious. They'd follow the footprints, trying to trace them back to their source. But the trail always ended at the lake, leaving them puzzled and slightly spooked. Rumors spread - tales of a ghostly swimmer who never made it to shore and now wanders the streets at dawn.

One day, a boy named Liam decided he'd solve the mystery once and for all. He camped out by the lake with a flashlight, determined to catch the phantom foot-traveler in the act. Hours passed, and the stillness of the night enveloped him. Just as he was about to drift into sleep, a splash broke the silence.

Liam aimed his flashlight toward the sound, and his heart raced as he saw a figure emerging from the water. The ghostly form slowly approached, leaving behind the familiar wet footprints. But as the figure drew closer, Liam realized it wasn't a ghost at all. It was an old man, with a long gray beard, dripping wet and shivering in the cold night air.

The man introduced himself as Mr. O'Reilly, a former resident of Willowbrook. Every year, he'd return to the town in the dead of night, take a swim in the lake, and walk back through town, revisiting memories of his youth. Liam and Mr. O'Reilly laughed at the town's wild imagination, and the next day, introduced the "ghost" of Willowbrook to everyone. From then on, the footprints were no longer a mystery, but they still appeared every year, reminding the town of its charming legend.

MYSTERIOUS MANSION

HAVE YOU EVER VENTURED INTO A PLACE YOU were told to stay away from? On the edge of town, atop a lonely hill, stood the abandoned Larkspur Mansion. It was said to be haunted, and no one dared to go near it after sunset. Grown-ups whispered tales of ghostly figures and strange noises, while children dared each other to approach its rusty gates.

One chilly autumn evening, three friends —Mia, Lucas, and Jake—summoned their courage and decided to explore the mansion. Armed with flashlights, they slowly approached the imposing structure. Its windows were dark and shattered, and ivy crawled up its stone walls.

Inside, they treaded carefully, their footsteps echoing in the vast hallways. Dusty portraits gazed down at them, and cobwebs hung in every corner. The deeper they went, the colder it got. Soon, they reached a grand ballroom. Its chandeliers swayed slightly, even though there was no wind. Then, a soft tune began to play from nowhere, growing louder and clearer: the sound of a piano.

The trio, gripping onto each other, followed the melody to a closed door. Lucas slowly turned the handle, and the room inside was shockingly well-preserved. A lit candelabra sat atop a grand piano, and sitting before it was a transparent figure of a lady in a long dress, her fingers gliding over the keys.

The children gasped. "Don't be afraid," she whispered, her voice soft and melodious. "I've been so lonely."

As the tale went, she was Lady Larkspur, waiting for her lost love to return. When he never did, she played the piano every night in sorrow.

Mia approached the piano and placed a

hand on it. The ghostly figure smiled grate-fully. "Thank you for visiting," she mur-mured, fading away, leaving only the soft glow of the candelabra.

The friends left the mansion with a story they'd never forget, realizing that not all ghosts were to be feared. Some just wanted to be heard.

THE APPARITION OF ROOM 313

Have you ever heard of a classroom that no one was allowed to enter? Room 313 at Maplewood Elementary had been locked for years. No one knew why, but rumors of a ghostly student trapped inside had spread throughout the school.

On a gloomy afternoon, Emma, Owen, and Lily found themselves near Room 313. Curiosity overcoming their fear, they decided to take a peek. To their surprise, the door was slightly ajar. Pushing it open, they discovered a classroom frozen in time. Dusty textbooks lay open, and an unfinished assignment remained on the chalkboard. The room was eerily silent except for the sound of their own heartbeats.

Suddenly, the door slammed shut behind them. The room grew colder, and a soft, otherworldly voice echoed, "I just want to finish my lesson."

Panicking, Owen tried to open the door but found it jammed. The room's temperature dropped further, and from the corner of her eye, Lily saw a faint figure of a boy dressed in old-fashioned clothes. He was hunched over a desk, scribbling away, seemingly unaware of their presence.

Emma, feeling an odd sense of calm, approached the apparition. "Who are you?" she asked gently.

The ghostly student looked up with sad eyes. "I'm Peter. I loved to learn, but I got sick one day and never returned. I just want to finish this lesson so I can rest."

Moved by Peter's story, Emma picked up a chalk piece. "Let's finish it together," she said.

As they worked through the math problem on the board, the atmosphere in Room 313 began to lighten. Once they solved the last equation, Peter smiled, his figure starting to fade. "Thank you," he whispered.

The door creaked open, revealing the hallway outside. The trio exited, a bit shaken but warmed by the knowledge that they'd helped a lost soul find peace. They never spoke of Room 313 again, but every now and then, they'd leave a new textbook by the door, just in case Peter wanted to learn something new.

CURSED LOCKET

HAVE YOU EVER WORN SOMETHING THAT seemed to transport you to another time? When Sofia stumbled upon an old, tarnished locket at a yard sale, she felt an immediate connection. Drawn to its intricate design, she placed it around her neck without a second thought.

That night, Sofia had the most vivid dream. She found herself in an old-fashioned ballroom, the air filled with laughter and music from a bygone era. Dressed in an elegant gown, she danced the night away with strangers. When she awoke, her room smelled faintly of roses and candle wax.

Throughout the week, more mysterious

events occurred. Sofia would catch glimpses of a woman in the mirror who wasn't her reflection but that of a lady from the past, with porcelain skin and hair styled in tight curls. The songs she had never heard before hummed in her mind, and she found herself writing letters with ink and quill, not even knowing to whom.

Growing uneasy, Sofia decided to research the locket. At the town library, she discovered a black and white photo of a woman who looked identical to the lady in her reflections, wearing the very same locket. The caption read: "Lady Isabella, who mysteriously vanished on the eve of her grand ball in 1875."

Chilled to the bone, Sofia realized the locket was trying to tell Lady Isabella's story. That night, she whispered to the locket, "Isabella, I want to help. Tell me what happened."

In her dream, Isabella appeared. "I lost my locket during the ball, and with it, a piece of my soul. I've been trapped ever since. Please, set me free."

Determined, Sofia took the locket to the very mansion where the ball had taken place, now a museum. In the ballroom, she opened the locket and out poured a radiant light. Lady Isabella's spirit danced one last time before peacefully fading away.

When Sofia woke up, the weight of the locket felt lighter. She knew Lady Isabella was finally free.

THE FORGOTTEN PLAYGROUND

HAVE YOU EVER STUMBLED UPON A PLACE THAT shouldn't be there? Deep in the woods behind Mia's new house lay a playground long forgotten. Tall trees shrouded it in shade, but what caught Mia's attention was the ancient swing set, its rusty chains groaning and seats swaying gently, even though there was no breeze.

Intrigued, Mia approached, drawn by the allure of the lonely swings. As she neared, she thought she heard soft whispers, like children giggling. A cold wind swirled around her, making the leaves rustle and the swings sway more violently.

"Who's there?" Mia called out, trying to

sound braver than she felt. No answer. Just the eerie sound of the chains creaking and those distant giggles.

Every day after school, Mia was drawn to the playground. She'd sit on a swing, feeling an invisible presence push her gently. The sensation was oddly comforting, like the touch of an old friend.

One evening, while the sun dipped behind the trees, casting long shadows, Mia saw translucent figures of children playing around her. They looked happy and carefree, their laughter more pronounced. One of them, a little girl with braided hair, beckoned Mia to join.

"Who are you?" Mia whispered.

"We're the children of time, forever playing," the little girl replied with a sad smile. "We were waiting for you."

Mia's heart raced. "Waiting for me?"

The ghostly girl nodded. "Every few years, someone like you discovers our playground. We just want to play and be remembered."

The next day, Mia returned with her friends. They played and laughed, making the old playground come alive once more.

The ghostly children faded away, their laughter mingling with that of the living kids.

Mia knew the secret of the forgotten playground: it wasn't haunted by spirits seeking revenge but by souls craving the joys of childhood. She made a promise to visit often, ensuring that the laughter would never fade away.

THE SILENT TELEPHONE

Have you ever heard a phone ring when it shouldn't? In the corner of Lucy's attic sat an old telephone, its cord cut and its once-shiny black surface now dusty and faded. Nobody remembered when it was last used or even where it came from. But every night, precisely at midnight, it would ring.

Lucy's first encounter with the phone was accidental. Seeking a forgotten toy, she ventured into the attic one night, just as the clock struck twelve. To her astonishment, the silent telephone began to ring loudly, its sound echoing eerily in the attic's silence.

Curiosity getting the better of her, Lucy approached the phone and, hesitating for just a moment, picked up the receiver. A chill ran down her spine as a raspy voice whispered, "Help me." The line then went dead.

Terrified, Lucy dropped the receiver and raced downstairs, swearing never to answer that phone again. But the next night, and the night after that, the phone rang at midnight. Lucy tried to ignore it, but the voice's plea haunted her dreams.

Determined to solve the mystery, Lucy told her grandfather about the phone. His eyes widened with recognition. "That phone," he murmured, "belonged to Mrs. Winters. She lived here many years ago and went missing. They never found her."

With renewed purpose, Lucy decided to communicate with the spirit. That night, she sat by the phone, waiting. As it rang, she took a deep breath and answered. "Mrs. Winters?" she ventured. The same raspy voice replied, "Help me find peace."

Lucy's heart raced. "How can I help?" she asked.

"Find my locket," the voice said. "In the garden, under the rosebush."

The next day, Lucy dug beneath the rosebush and unearthed a beautiful locket. Inside was a photo of Mrs. Winters. That night, the phone remained silent.

From then on, Lucy wore the locket in memory of the spirit she'd helped and the phone that rang no more.

CLOCK TOWER MYSTERY

HAVE YOU EVER HEARD A CLOCK STRIKE thirteen times? In the town of Eldridge, the ancient clock tower did just that every night, and no one knew why. As legend had it, when the clock chimed its mysterious thirteenth toll, it marked the beginning of a ghostly gathering.

Young Max was a curious boy, and he couldn't resist the lure of the legend. One evening, armed with a flashlight and bolstered by his own daring spirit, he ventured to the town square just before midnight.

The night was dark and chilly. Fog blanketed the streets, and the only sound was the distant hoot of an owl. As Max approached the clock tower, he noticed its hands were nearing the top of the hour. His heart raced in anticipation.

Suddenly, the clock started its chime. Each bong resonated through the quiet night. When the twelfth chime faded, Max held his breath. Then, to his astonishment, a hauntingly slow thirteenth chime rang out.

With that eerie sound, the ground around the clock tower began to shimmer and waver. Slowly, translucent figures materialized, swirling around like a silent dance of wraiths. Their attire looked old-fashioned, and they seemed to be communicating with each other, though no words were heard.

Max's fear melted into wonder. He realized these ghosts were the spirits of the town's founders, who returned every night to discuss the welfare of Eldridge. One spirit, a lady in a long, flowing gown, noticed Max and floated towards him. She smiled kindly, "Fear not, young one. We mean no harm. We simply care for our beloved town, even in death."

As the first rays of dawn began to appear,

the spirits faded away, leaving Max with a tale no one would believe. But he knew the truth about the thirteenth chime and the guardians of Eldridge who convened beneath the clock tower.

BEHIND THE BOOKSHELF

HAVE YOU EVER FOUND A ROOM THAT ISN'T supposed to exist? In the old house that Ellie moved into, a bookshelf held secrets beyond anyone's wildest imagination.

Ellie loved reading and was thrilled to see a grand bookshelf in her new room. One day, while searching for a bedtime story, she noticed a peculiar book titled, "Midnight Tales." Trying to pull it out, she was surprised when the bookshelf creaked and slowly swung open, revealing a hidden chamber.

The chamber was filled with ancient books, each with gleaming titles that promised adventures and mysteries. But the room had an unusual rule inscribed on a plaque: "Read by day, but leave be at night."

That evening, as Ellie lay in bed, she heard soft whispers coming from the direction of the secret room. Curiosity got the better of her, and she tiptoed to the entrance. Peeking in, she saw the books quivering and shaking on their shelves. Then, one by one, they opened, releasing shimmering figures into the room. Pirates, princesses, dragons, and other characters from the pages began to interact, reenacting their stories.

Ellie was entranced. The tales she had loved reading were coming to life before her eyes! But soon, she noticed one ghostly figure lingering near the entrance, a storyteller from an old legend, who seemed to be searching for something. Their eyes met, and Ellie felt a chill. "Lost stories must find their way back," he murmured, reaching out towards her.

Panicking, Ellie remembered the warning. She quickly grabbed "Midnight Tales" and placed it back on its shelf. As she did, the figures began returning to their books, including the storyteller. The room fell silent once more.

From that night on, Ellie respected the room's rule. She realized some stories were meant to be read, but others had a life of their own, waiting for the cover of darkness to live out their tales.

THE GHOST'S DIARY

HAVE YOU EVER READ A STORY THAT FELT JUST a bit too real? Tom stumbled upon such a tale one rainy afternoon.

In the attic of his family's ancestral home, Tom found a dusty old diary, its pages yellowed with age. The leather cover simply read, "Eleanor's Memoirs." Curious, he began to flip through, reading about a young girl named Eleanor who had lived in the same house hundreds of years ago.

The entries detailed Eleanor's life, her joys, her sorrows, and her mysteries. But as Tom read on, he noticed something peculiar. The diary's dates didn't end in the past; they continued up to today and even hinted at tomorrow.

Tonight's entry read, "The rain mirrors my loneliness. But today, I felt a presence. Someone's here, reading my life."

Tom shivered, glancing around the dim attic. He heard the subtle sound of quill scratching on paper and turned back to the diary. To his astonishment, words began to form on the next empty page: "Hello, Tom."

Gasping, he dropped the diary. The quill continued to move, writing, "Don't be afraid. It's only me, Eleanor."

Gathering his courage, Tom whispered, "Are you... real?"

The quill danced gracefully, forming the words, "As real as the memories on these pages."

He hesitated, then asked, "Why are you writing to me?"

"I've been waiting for someone to share my story with," came Eleanor's reply. "Now that you've found my diary, we can finally meet."

Suddenly, a soft glow illuminated a corner of the attic, revealing a translucent figure of a young girl, her eyes kind. "Hello,

Tom," Eleanor whispered, her voice echoing through the ages.

From that day on, the two formed an unlikely friendship. Tom would read, and Eleanor would write, ensuring her tale would never be forgotten. And while others might've been terrified, Tom had found a connection that transcended time.

MOONLIT REFLECTIONS

HAVE YOU EVER WONDERED IF THERE'S another world hidden in the shadows? Every full moon, the residents of Willowville got a glimpse of one.

The local children often camped by the edge of Willowville's pristine lake, listening to the crickets and watching the moonlight dance on the water. But they were always warned not to stay out too late on full moon nights. Curious as children are, one night, Jenny and Max decided they needed to uncover the truth behind the tales.

The night was clear, and the full moon hung brightly in the sky, casting a silver glow on the lake. As midnight approached, the calm waters began to ripple. The reflections changed, showing not the trees and sky of Willowville, but a ghostly town with old, decrepit buildings, and shadowy figures roaming around.

Jenny gasped, "Look, Max! The reflections! It's like... a different world!"

The shadowy figures seemed to notice them too, pointing and whispering among themselves. One figure, clearer than the rest, began walking towards the water's edge, its gaze fixed on the two children. Jenny and Max clutched each other, their hearts racing.

As the figure touched the water, it began to rise, materializing from the lake, water dripping from its transparent form. It was a woman in an old-fashioned gown, her eyes kind but sorrowful.

"I mean no harm," she whispered. "We're trapped in this reflection, bound to the moon's glow, a memory of Willowville's past."

Jenny, gathering courage, asked, "How can we help?"

"You already have," replied the ghostly figure. "By seeing and acknowledging us, you've given our spirits solace."

The night lightened as dawn approached, and the ghostly apparitions faded back into the lake, leaving only the reflections of trees and stars.

Jenny and Max realized the importance of remembering and honoring the past. And while the ghostly visions on full moon nights continued, the children of Willowville always greeted them with a wave, a bridge between the worlds.

PHANTOM'S MELODY

HAVE YOU EVER HEARD A TUNE THAT SENDS shivers down your spine? In the attic of the Morgan family's new house, a dusty old piano held a mysterious secret.

The first night they moved in, Emily, a curious 10-year-old, was awakened by the haunting sound of a piano. Following the music, she found herself in the attic, staring at the old instrument. But there was no one there. How could a piano play on its own?

As nights went on, the melody became more complex and beautiful, capturing Emily's imagination. She tried to play the tune during the day, but her fingers just couldn't replicate the ghostly composition. She became obsessed with unraveling the mystery behind the music.

One evening, she decided to stay up and hide in the attic. Midnight struck, and the piano's keys began to move. Suddenly, a transparent figure appeared, hovering above the piano bench. It was a gentleman dressed in old-fashioned attire, passionately guiding the keys with elegance.

Entranced, Emily whispered, "Who are you?"

The ghostly figure paused and looked at her with sorrowful eyes. "I am Richard, a composer from a century ago. I was creating my magnum opus, but before I could finish, I met my untimely end. I return, hoping to complete it."

Emily, with a heart full of sympathy, replied, "I want to help. Teach me."

Under Richard's guidance, Emily practiced every day, becoming the vessel for his unfinished symphony. The townspeople were amazed at her prodigious talent.

On the night of a grand recital, as Emily played the phantom's melody, Richard appeared beside her, playing in harmony. The climax of the tune was breathtaking, and the room erupted in applause. With a smile and a nod, Richard's spirit faded away, finally at peace.

The old piano, having served its purpose, never played on its own again. But Emily always felt the presence of her ghostly maestro, guiding her fingers in every performance.

THE HAUNTING OF
HALLWAY 6

HAVE YOU EVER WALKED DOWN A HALLWAY that felt like it would never end? At Millbrook Elementary, there was one such corridor—Hallway 6.

Rumors swirled among students about Hallway 6. Some said that at night, it became a bridge to a ghostly realm. Others whispered of seeing shadowy figures. No one dared to venture there after sunset.

One evening, as a dare, Mia and her friends decided to explore Hallway 6. Armed with flashlights, they tiptoed into the school. The moonlight barely illuminated the entrance to the infamous corridor.

As they walked, the hallway seemed to

stretch longer and longer, the walls shifting and echoing with whispered voices from times long gone. The flashlights flickered, and the temperature dropped, making their breath visible.

Suddenly, classroom doors creaked open, revealing empty rooms where ghostly lessons took place. Phantasmal teachers pointed to chalkboards, while spectral students scribbled notes. Mia and her friends were captivated, witnessing the past come alive.

But then, a distinct voice reached Mia's ears. "Why are you here?" The voice belonged to a young girl, wearing an old-fashioned school uniform. She stood at the end of the hallway, her eyes filled with curiosity.

Mia mustered courage and replied, "We wanted to see if the stories were true."

The ghostly girl chuckled. "Many venture here out of curiosity, but few see our world. You are special." With a wave of her hand, the apparitions vanished, leaving behind an ordinary hallway.

The group, heartbeats racing, raced out of the school, grateful for the moonlit night outside. They never spoke of that night again, but Mia often felt the ghostly girl's presence, watching over her.

To this day, Hallway 6 remains an unsolved mystery at Millbrook Elementary. But for those who believe, it's a reminder that some doors, once opened, bridge the gap between two realms.

SLEEPY HOLLOW CAMPGROUNDS

HAVE YOU EVER HEARD A CAMPFIRE TALE SO real that it sent chills down your spine? At Sleepy Hollow Campgrounds, legends become reality.

Every summer, eager campers arrived, ready for adventure. They pitched tents, roasted marshmallows, and as night fell, they would gather around the campfire to share tales. The most popular story was about the Ghostly Wanderer, a spirit said to roam the campgrounds, searching for his lost love.

One night, a group of friends, Lucas, Eliza, and Sam, were sharing this very story. They spoke of the Wanderer's mournful cries and the rustling leaves that signaled his approach.

As Lucas narrated, the wind began to howl, and the flames flickered erratically. Suddenly, a chilling wail pierced the air, making everyone jump. They tried to laugh it off, thinking it was another camper trying to scare them.

But then, they noticed a silhouette emerging from the dense forest. It was a man, draped in tattered clothes, his face hidden under a wide-brimmed hat. The trio's hearts raced as they realized it matched the description of the Ghostly Wanderer.

Eliza, trying to be brave, called out, "Is this a prank? It's not funny!"

But the figure didn't respond. Instead, it pointed to an old, worn-out locket lying on the ground. Lucas picked it up, revealing a portrait of a beautiful woman inside. The Wanderer's cries grew louder, filled with agony.

Suddenly, another ghostly figure appeared—a woman, radiating a soft glow. She approached the Wanderer, and as their hands touched, they both vanished, leaving behind a serene silence.

The campers sat in awe, realizing they had witnessed the reunion of two lost souls.

From that day on, the Ghostly Wanderer's cries were never heard again at Sleepy Hollow Campgrounds. But campers continued to share their eerie tale, a testament to the power of love that transcended even the boundaries of life and death.

THE WITCH'S PORTRAIT

HAVE YOU EVER FELT LIKE SOMEONE WAS watching you, even when you were alone? Sarah did, and it all started with an old painting she found in her grandmother's attic.

Sarah was playing hide-and-seek with her cousin Jack when she stumbled upon a dusty old portrait of a stern-looking woman dressed in dark, old-fashioned clothes. But what really caught her attention were the woman's eyes—they seemed so lifelike, so intense.

"That's the old witch of Willowbrook," Jack whispered when he saw the painting.

"They say she was a powerful sorceress who could communicate through her portrait."

Sarah laughed it off, thinking Jack was just trying to scare her. But that night, as she lay in bed, she felt an odd sensation. It felt as though someone was watching her.

She glanced at the portrait, which now hung in her room. To her astonishment, the witch's eyes seemed to be following her every move. A cold shiver ran down her spine. Was the tale Jack told true?

The next evening, as Sarah was studying, she heard a faint whisper coming from the painting. "Help... me..." the voice pleaded. The witch's eyes were filled with sadness and desperation.

Not sure if it was real or her imagination, Sarah approached the portrait. "What do you want?" she bravely asked.

"Release... me," the voice responded. "Find... the locket."

With growing determination, Sarah searched the attic and found an old locket buried beneath some books. As she opened it, a gust of wind blew in, and the portrait's image changed. The witch's stern face was now smiling, her eyes filled with gratitude.

The following morning, Sarah found a note where the portrait once hung: "Thank you for setting me free. - Willowbrook Witch."

Sarah realized the power of legends and the importance of helping, even if it meant aiding a witch trapped in a portrait.

THE LOST TRAIN OF BLACKWOOD

HAVE YOU EVER HEARD A TRAIN WHISTLE IN the dead of night when there are no tracks nearby? In the town of Blackwood, it wasn't just a sound—it was a legend.

Legend had it that many years ago, a train disappeared into the dense Blackwood forest. Every night at midnight, its haunting whistle could be heard, echoing through the woods as it searched for its missing conductor.

Tommy and Lucy, two brave siblings, decided one fateful night to uncover the truth. Armed with a lantern and their curiosity, they ventured into the forest, guided by the eerie whistle.

As the clock neared midnight, a thick mist enveloped the trees. Suddenly, bright lights pierced through the fog, and the kids saw the ghostly silhouette of a train. It shimmered and flickered as if caught between two worlds.

Drawn to its mystery, Tommy and Lucy climbed aboard. Inside, they found everything perfectly preserved, as though time had frozen. But what caught their attention was a forlorn figure in the conductor's cabin.

A translucent man, the ghostly conductor, turned to them, his eyes filled with sadness. "I lost my way," he whispered, "and with it, my train and my passengers. Can you help me find my path?"

Realizing that the train and its conductor were trapped in limbo, the children decided to help. Recalling an old town map they'd seen, they guided the conductor through the forest's trails. After what felt like hours, they arrived at a forgotten railway track.

The moment the train touched the rails, it solidified. The ghostly passengers inside began to wake, smiling and chatting. The conductor, with tears in his eyes, thanked the children, and as the clock struck dawn, the train chugged away, finally on its rightful path.

From that day on, the midnight whistle ceased. But the tale of Tommy, Lucy, and the Lost Train of Blackwood became an enduring legend.

NIGHTMARE AT NORTH STREET

HAVE YOU EVER FELT THE CHILL OF A GHOSTLY tale creeping into reality? On North Street, an age-old legend came chillingly alive for Mia, Jake, and Zoe.

The trio had always been fascinated by the legend of the ghostly carriage. Whispers spoke of a phantom carriage drawn by dark horses, appearing on North Street at midnight. It was said to transport the souls of those who dared to sit inside.

One windy evening, as clouds concealed the moon, the friends decided to challenge the legend. Standing on North Street, they nervously awaited the midnight hour. The wind whispered secrets, and the night grew colder.

Suddenly, the rhythmic sound of hooves clattered in the distance. The friends exchanged terrified glances as a shadowy figure emerged—a carriage drawn by inky-black horses, driven by a cloaked figure with hollow eyes. The legend was real!

Determined not to back down, Mia stepped forward, her voice trembling, "We challenge the legend!" The driver nodded, and the carriage doors creaked open. Swallowing their fear, the trio stepped inside.

The inside was luxurious but cold. Velvet seats, silver accents, and an eerie blue glow. Before they could react, the carriage bolted forward, taking them on a wild journey through time and memories.

Houses transformed into ruins and back again, and faces from their past flashed outside the windows. It was both magical and terrifying. Suddenly, Zoe realized that none of the legends mentioned how to return!

In a moment of clarity, Mia remembered an old rhyme about North Street's ghostly carriage. Joining hands, the trio chanted,

"Past the memories, through the fright, take us back to North Street's light!"

The carriage jolted and halted abruptly. The door swung open to reveal North Street, just as they remembered. The phantom driver tipped his hat, and with a ghostly whistle, the carriage vanished.

The friends were left stunned, forever bound by the night they turned legend into reality. The Nightmare at North Street became their own tale to tell, with a cautionary note to respect the mysteries of the past.

BENEATH THE BASEMENT

EVER WONDER WHAT MYSTERIES HIDE BENEATH your feet? Max's ordinary Saturday turned extraordinary when his quest for a lost toy led him to an ancient trapdoor in his basement.

Curiosity piqued, Max decided to pry open the heavy wooden door, revealing a stone staircase descending into darkness. Armed with a flashlight, he ventured down, each step echoing through the silence. The staircase ended at a long, dim tunnel. Hesitant but intrigued, Max followed it.

The tunnel opened up to reveal a sight Max could scarcely believe—an entire ghost town, right beneath his house! Dusty roads, derelict buildings, a silent saloon, and an abandoned town square all lay in shadow. But something felt... off. The town wasn't entirely empty.

As Max wandered, he began to hear faint whispers, the distant sound of laughter, and a piano playing a haunting tune. Shadows danced on the walls, and he felt eyes watching him. Suddenly, a playful gust of wind blew his cap off, leading him to an old schoolhouse. Hesitant, Max stepped inside.

Rows of transparent children sat at wooden desks, their ghostly eyes fixed on a specter teacher who looked up as Max entered. "Ah! A new student!" she exclaimed. The ghostly children giggled.

Panicking, Max backed away, only to be surrounded by the spirits of the townsfolk. They whispered tales of a forgotten town that once thrived above ground but was buried after a massive earthquake. They were the souls left behind.

Max, mustering his courage, spoke, "I can tell your story! Let the world know about this hidden town beneath my basement!" The ghosts murmured in agreement. The spectral teacher handed him an old journal, filled with the town's history.

With the journal in hand, Max retraced his steps, climbing up the staircase and sealing the trapdoor. The next day, he shared the journal's tales with his family, ensuring the ghost town's legacy lived on.

And sometimes, late at night, Max would hear the distant sound of a piano, thanking him for remembering.

THE CURSED AMULET

HAVE YOU EVER WISHED FOR A GIFT THAT turned out to be a curse? On her tenth birthday, Lily received an unexpected present from her mysterious old aunt—a shimmering amulet with a deep blue gem.

Excitedly, Lily clasped it around her neck. As soon as the amulet touched her skin, the world shifted. Her once-familiar room became alive with ethereal figures— spirits of all shapes and sizes, floating, whispering, lamenting.

At first, Lily was fascinated. She spoke to the spirits and heard tales of bygone eras. But as the days passed, the novelty wore off. The spirits never left her side, and their constant presence became overbearing. The whispers turned into cries, and the gentle figures became more demanding. They wanted her to help them with their unresolved tasks, from finding lost possessions to delivering messages to loved ones.

Sleep-deprived and desperate, Lily decided she had to remove the amulet. But no matter how hard she tried, it wouldn't come off. Each tug was met with louder cries from the spirits, their ghostly fingers reaching out to her.

One night, in the midst of her desperation, a kind spirit appeared—a little girl about Lily's age. "The amulet is cursed," she whispered, her voice melodic yet sad. "But there is a way to break its power. You must return it to its resting place."

Guided by the ghostly girl, Lily ventured to an old graveyard where a statue of an angel held its hand out, waiting. Placing the amulet in the statue's hand, Lily felt an immediate relief. The spirits faded, leaving her in peaceful solitude.

The little spirit girl smiled, "Thank you, Lily." And just before vanishing, she whispered, "The amulet was my curse too, once."

Grateful and free, Lily returned home, knowing she'd never wish for such a "gift" again. She'd learned that not all that glitters is gold—some are shadows of the past, yearning to be set free.

ECHOES OF THE OPERA

EVER HEARD MUSIC WHERE THERE SHOULDN'T be any? In the heart of the town stood the abandoned Greystone Opera House, a relic of a bygone era. Children were warned not to venture near it, especially at night. But Sarah, an inquisitive 11-year-old, was drawn to its haunting beauty.

One evening, Sarah's curiosity got the better of her. Armed with just a flashlight, she tiptoed into the opera house. Cobwebs clung to velvet seats, and dust covered the grand stage. Yet, it felt... alive.

As she explored, the strangest thing happened—the soft strains of an orchestra tuning their instruments filled the air. A spotlight suddenly shone on the stage, revealing an elegant ballerina. She danced gracefully, her moves perfectly synchronized with the melancholic tune of a phantom orchestra. Entranced, Sarah couldn't believe her eyes. Was this a performance from another time?

Suddenly, the ballerina paused and looked straight at Sarah, beckoning her. Sarah hesitated but felt a strange urge to join her. The music grew louder, more urgent, and as she climbed onto the stage, the entire opera house came to life. Ghostly figures filled the audience seats, applauding and cheering.

The ballerina whispered, "Dance with me, and be a part of the eternal opera." Sarah felt a shiver down her spine, realizing that she might be trapped in this ghostly performance forever.

Mustering courage, she replied, "I appreciate your dance, but I belong to my own time." As she spoke, she noticed a dusty old gramophone on the side of the stage. Racing to it, she turned it off, and instantly, the music ceased. The ghostly figures, including the ballerina, faded away, leaving Sarah alone in the eerie silence.

Catching her breath, Sarah hurried out, vowing never to return. The Greystone Opera House had given its last performance, at least for her. But every time she heard the haunting strains of a violin or the soft tap of ballet shoes, she remembered her dance with the specters of the past.

GHOSTLY GARDEN

HAVE YOU EVER HEARD A STATUE WHISPER? Mia did. It was a sunny afternoon when she stumbled upon an overgrown, forgotten garden tucked behind her new house. Enchanted by its wild beauty, Mia ventured deeper, finding statues of various shapes and sizes.

As she admired a stone fairy with delicate wings, Mia thought she heard a soft whisper: "Find her..." She spun around, looking for the source, but saw no one. Chalking it up to her imagination, she continued her exploration.

But then she heard it again, from a moss-covered gnome this time, "Uncover the tale..."

Intrigued, Mia decided to play along. "What tale?" she asked aloud.

A chorus of whispers filled the air, guiding her towards a corner of the garden where a majestic willow tree stood. Beneath it was a statue of a young girl, different from the rest. It looked... sad.

"Help her," the statues whispered. Mia approached, and as she did, a gust of wind rustled the willow's leaves, revealing a hidden plaque. It read: "Liliana, the lost girl of the garden."

Mia's heart raced. She felt an overwhelming urge to help Liliana. Searching around the statue, she found a small, locked chest. As she touched it, the whispers grew louder, guiding her to find the key. Following the statue's hints, she located the key beneath a pile of stones.

Unlocking the chest, Mia discovered a diary. It belonged to Liliana, who had once lived in Mia's house and loved the garden. But she was unfairly accused of mischief and banned from her beloved garden. Heartbroken, she left, never to return.

Realizing the statues were the spirits of the garden, trying to share Liliana's story,

Mia decided to honor her. She cleaned and restored the garden, placing Liliana's statue at its center.

That night, Mia heard one last whisper, "Thank you." The statues were silent after that, but Mia often felt a gentle presence, watching over her as she played, forever grateful for the story she had uncovered.

THE MIRROR MAZE

HAVE YOU EVER SEEN A REFLECTION THAT wasn't yours? Jake did. Excitement bubbled within him as he stepped into the carnival's famed mirror maze. Neon lights illuminated the countless mirrors that stretched in every direction.

But as Jake ventured deeper, the reflections became... odd. Instead of his blue t-shirt and sneakers, some mirrors showed a boy in old-fashioned clothes—a white shirt, suspenders, and worn-out boots. Confused, Jake touched the mirror, half expecting his hand to pass through to another world.

Suddenly, a hushed whisper floated through the maze. "Find me, Jake," it urged.

Jake's heart pounded in his chest. Determined to solve the mystery, he followed the voice. The maze twisted and turned, the reflections changing from one era to another. Women in long gowns, men in top hats, children in ruffled dresses, all echoed in the maze, watching Jake with expectant eyes.

With every turn, the voice grew louder. "Closer, Jake... closer..."

Finally, Jake stood before a mirror, different from the rest. Its frame was ornate, and the glass shimmered with an otherworldly glow. The reflection showed a boy, identical to Jake, but dressed in clothes from a century ago. Their eyes met.

"I am James," the reflection whispered. "I was lost in this maze, trapped between reflections of the past. But now, you've found me."

A gust of wind blew through the maze, and the mirrors rippled like water. When everything settled, Jake saw only his own reflection staring back. The maze had returned to normal, but Jake would never forget James, his mirror twin from the past.

As Jake exited the maze, an old carnival worker nodded at him. "You've met James, haven't you?" he asked with a knowing smile. "Every once in a while, he finds someone to remind him he's not forgotten." Jake shivered, the carnival's music taking on a haunting tune as he walked away.

SPECTER ON THE STAIRS

HAVE YOU EVER CLIMBED A STAIRCASE THAT seemed to go on forever? At the heart of the old Redwood Mansion, a grand spiral staircase stretched upwards, touching tales of romance and mystery.

Sarah, an adventurous girl of eleven, had heard whispers about the mansion. Rumor had it that a specter haunted the steps, endlessly seeking its lost love. One fateful evening, curiosity pulled Sarah to the mansion's heavy wooden doors.

As she placed her foot on the first step, a soft, melancholic tune played on a distant piano. The air grew cold, and the candle chandelier above flickered. Sarah hesitated but continued climbing. With every step, she felt a growing presence.

Suddenly, a translucent figure appeared —a young woman in a flowing gown, her eyes filled with tears. She drifted from one step to another, her fingers brushing the wooden railings. "Edward," she whispered, her voice echoing in the vast hall.

Sarah mustered courage. "Who are you?"

The specter turned, her eyes locking onto Sarah's. "I am Eleanor. I waited for my love, Edward, to return from war. But he never did. Now, I roam these stairs, hoping to find him."

Sarah's heart ached for the lost lovers. She remembered a portrait she'd seen downstairs of a soldier named Edward. "I think I know where he is," she said, leading Eleanor to the grand hall.

The two stood before Edward's portrait. As Eleanor reached out to touch the painting, it transformed, revealing a hidden compartment. Inside was a letter, yellowed with age. It was from Edward, expressing his undying love for Eleanor.

Eleanor's ghostly form shimmered with joy. The air warmed, and the mansion seemed to breathe a sigh of relief. "Thank you," she whispered, before fading away, finally united with her lost love in spirit.

Sarah left the mansion, its haunting tales replaced with a story of love, hope, and reunion.

THE HAUNTED
HOMEWORK

EVER FOUND SOMETHING IN YOUR TEXTBOOK that didn't belong there? One chilly afternoon, Max opened his old math textbook to find a piece of paper nestled between the pages. The assignment, faded and crinkled, was titled, "Mysteries of Numbers," and bore the name 'Lucas W.'

Curiosity piqued, Max started reading the questions. They weren't like regular math problems. "If a ghost flies at 3 mph, how long does it take to haunt a castle 9 miles away?" Another read, "Calculate the number of souls in a haunted house if each room has 7."

Max felt a shiver, but his curiosity urged

him on. He decided to complete the assignment for fun. However, as he started solving, strange things happened. His pencil would move on its own, writing answers he hadn't thought of. Shadows danced on the walls, taking the shape of numbers.

Suddenly, the room grew icy cold. From the corner of his eye, Max saw a pale figure: a boy with old-fashioned clothes, looking distressed. "Lucas?" Max whispered.

The ghostly figure nodded. "I couldn't finish the assignment. It's my one regret," Lucas murmured. "It kept me tied to this world."

Max gulped, gathering his courage. "Let's solve it together," he proposed.

Together, they worked through the mysterious math problems. With each answer, Lucas became more transparent, more at peace. Finally, when the last question was solved, Lucas smiled gratefully. "Thank you," he whispered, vanishing into thin air, leaving behind a room that suddenly felt warmer and brighter.

The next day, Max handed in the assignment. His teacher, surprised, explained that 'Mysteries of Numbers' was an assignment from decades ago. "Lucas W.," she mused, "was a student who loved mysteries but disappeared before completing this one."

Max smiled, thinking of Lucas. The haunted homework was no longer a mystery, and somewhere, a spirit was finally free.

MYSTIC MUSEUM

HAVE YOU EVER WONDERED IF MUSEUMS HOLD secrets beyond what meets the eye? On a gray morning, Mrs. Jensen's class arrived at the Mystic Museum. From ancient relics to forgotten artifacts, it promised a journey through time. But there was one room that wasn't on the itinerary: The Chamber of Haunted History.

A sign on the chamber's door read: "Enter if you dare." Eva, Max, and Leo, the trio of adventurous friends, exchanged a mischievous glance. Slipping away from the group, they decided to explore.

Inside, the chamber was dimly lit, casting eerie shadows on the walls. The exhibits were unlike any they'd seen. A painting depicted a grand ballroom where ghostly figures danced eternally. A vintage mirror showed reflections of people who weren't in the room. An old grandfather clock ticked away, but its hands moved backward.

Suddenly, a whisper echoed, "Unravel the stories, or forever remain."

The trio exchanged worried glances. "We need to solve the mystery of these exhibits," whispered Eva, her voice quivering.

In the corner, they found a dusty old book titled "Stories of the Haunted." Flipping through, they discovered tales of souls trapped within the exhibits, yearning for their stories to be told.

Working together, the kids read aloud each story. With every tale, an exhibit would come alive, revealing its ghostly resident. The dancing figures in the painting swirled joyously before fading away. The mirror's phantom reflections smiled, nodding in gratitude. The clock's chimes rang out, and as its hands corrected their course, the room grew brighter.

As the final story was recited, the mysterious whisper returned: "Thank you." The chamber door creaked open, revealing the astonished faces of Mrs. Jensen and the class. Eva, Max, and Leo exited, the chamber's secrets safe with them. They'd learned that every relic has a tale, and sometimes, just sometimes, they might be hauntingly real.

GLOWING GRAVES

HAVE YOU EVER WALKED BY A CEMETERY AND felt a shiver down your spine? In the town of Hollow Hill, there was one cemetery that held a radiant secret.

Every year, on the eve of All Hallows' Day, a few curious children would notice an eerie glow emanating from the cemetery. It wasn't from lamps or moonlight; it was the tombstones themselves! They shimmered in brilliant shades of blue, green, and purple.

Tommy, Lily, and Sam, three close friends, decided they had to uncover the mystery behind the glowing graves. Armed with a flashlight, a notepad, and an unyielding sense of adventure, they snuck in one chilly October night.

As they navigated the maze of gravestones, the glow became more pronounced. Soon, they reached the heart of the cemetery, where the brightest tombstones stood. But it wasn't just the stones that caught their attention. Around these graves, translucent figures danced, laughed, and chatted. It was a spectral soiree!

Hiding behind a large oak tree, the trio watched in awe. They saw the spirits sharing stories of their past lives, reuniting with old friends, and even playing ghostly games.

Suddenly, an elderly ghost, her hair flowing like silver mist, approached the children. "Why are you here?" she asked gently.

"We...we wanted to see the glowing graves," Lily stammered.

The ghost smiled warmly. "These are the graves of those who left behind unfinished stories. Every year, we gather to share our tales and bask in the glow of memories. Tonight, we have special guests." She beckoned the children forward.

Tommy, Lily, and Sam hesitated but then joined the circle of spirits. For a brief moment, they felt an overwhelming sense of love and nostalgia.

As dawn approached, the glow began to fade. The spirits waved goodbye, and the children left, their hearts full of stories they'd never forget.

The glowing graves of Hollow Hill were no longer just a mystery; they were a reminder of the tales that connect the past and the present.

THE ABANDONED AMUSEMENT PARK

HAVE YOU EVER WONDERED WHAT HAPPENS IN an abandoned amusement park when everyone's asleep? In the small town of Larkspur, a legend whispered that the old Whispering Woods Park came alive once a year. On the outskirts of town, past the dense woods, the rusted entrance of the park stood silent. But every year, on the anniversary of its closure, brave kids dared each other to venture inside.

One year, Mia, Jay, and Luke, filled with youthful courage, decided to see if the legends were true. As the sun set, they hesitantly entered the park. The atmosphere was heavy with silence, only broken by the soft whisper of the trees.

Suddenly, the merry-go-round creaked to life, its worn-out horses moving up and down, illuminated by an eerie, pale glow. Ghostly laughter echoed as transparent children hopped onto the ride. The Ferris wheel began turning slowly, its cabins filled with shadowy figures that waved cheerfully. A spectral tune played from the forgotten arcade, luring the trio deeper into the park.

Heart pounding, Mia whispered, "Do you think they're... real?"

Before anyone could answer, a translucent figure appeared before them. It was Mr. Whitman, the old park owner. "Ah! Some living guests! It's been ages," he chuckled. "Care for a ride?"

Overcoming their initial fear, the kids hesitantly agreed. They rode the phantom roller coaster, which sent thrilling chills down their spines, and danced to the ghostly tunes.

As dawn approached, the rides began to slow, and the ghostly apparitions faded away. Mr. Whitman, with a twinkle in his transparent eyes, said, "Thank you for visiting. Remember, we're only here once a year."

The kids rushed home, their minds buzzing with wonder. The legend of Whispering Woods Park was true! And every year, they'd be first in line, eagerly awaiting the night when the ghostly rides woke up once more.

SPECTRAL SCHOOL BUS

HAVE YOU EVER WONDERED WHERE GHOSTLY children go to learn and play? In the town of Greenwood, the answer might surprise you.

Every autumn morning, as the fog rolled in, the children at Greenwood Elementary whispered about the mysterious old bus that roamed the streets. Unlike other buses, this one was faded with chipped paint, and its headlights glowed an unsettling shade of blue.

One day, curious siblings Jake and Lucy decided to follow the rumors. They hid behind the tall oak tree at the corner of Maple Street, waiting for the spectral bus.

Just as the stories described, a ghostly

bus with a dim number "40" appeared, its engine humming softly. Shadowy figures of children could be seen inside, their laughter echoing eerily. The doors creaked open, and a translucent driver beckoned. "Want to join? We're headed to Ashwood School."

Jake and Lucy exchanged nervous glances. The town had no "Ashwood School." It was said to have burned down decades ago. Gathering courage, the siblings stepped onto the bus.

Inside, they were greeted by children dressed in old-fashioned clothes, chatting and playing games. The bus rode through foggy landscapes before stopping in front of an imposing, ancient-looking school building.

Feeling out of place, Jake and Lucy tried to mingle. They learned that Ashwood School was a haven for spirits, a place to re-live their favorite school moments. The ghostly children were kind, sharing tales of days gone by.

However, as sunset approached, the ghostly headmistress approached the siblings. "You mustn't stay," she whispered. "This place isn't for the living."

With a rush of wind, Jake and Lucy found themselves back at Maple Street. The Spectral School Bus was nowhere in sight, but the memories of their ghostly adventure would remain forever.

From that day on, whenever the children at Greenwood Elementary spoke of the ghostly bus, Jake and Lucy would smile knowingly, cherishing the secret of the lost Ashwood School.

Made in the USA
Las Vegas, NV
04 November 2024

11158294R00059